The Headmaster Disaster

by Katie Dale and Sarah Hoyle

W
FRANKLIN WATTS
LONDON•SYDNEY

Tommy was always getting Sam into trouble.

"Who threw that rubber?" the Headmaster,

Mr Brown, said in assembly.

"Sam did," Tommy fibbed.

"No I didn't – it was Tommy!" Sam said.

"Don't tell fibs, Sam," Mr Brown said.

"The rubber has your name on it. Stay inside

at break time."

Sam frowned. Tommy must have written

Sam's name on the rubber!

"It's so unfair," Sam moaned to Gran.

"Mr Brown never believes me. He hates me!"

"When I was at school, if I wanted a teacher
to like me, I gave them an apple," Gran said,
giving Sam an apple from her fruit bowl.

"Thanks," said Sam. "I hope it works."

The next day, Sam took the apple to school.

In assembly, Tommy put up his hand. "Mr Brown, Sam's eating an apple," he said.

"No eating in assembly!" Mr Brown snapped. "Come here, Sam."

Sam walked to the front.

"I wasn't eating it," Sam explained. "The apple is for you, Mr Brown."

"For me?" said Mr Brown, surprised.

"Well ... thank you." He took a large bite.

Then something strange happened ...

Sam and Mr Brown swapped bodies!

"What's happened?" Mr Brown gasped

in Sam's voice.

"I don't know," Sam said – in a deep voice.

He stared down at his long legs and huge feet,

then he looked at the apple in his big hand.

It must be magic!

Sam grinned. Being Headmaster could be fun.
"Let's play some pop music," he said, turning
the radio on. "Who wants to sing and dance?"
Everyone cheered and danced and sang along
... except Mr Brown. "Stop!" Mr Brown said.
"Turn it off! You can't play pop music in
assembly!"

"I can do whatever I like," Sam smiled. "After all, I'm the Headmaster."

"No you're not, I'm the Headmaster!" Mr Brown said.

Everyone gasped.

"Don't tell fibs, Sam," said Sam. "Sit down now please."

Mr Brown stared at him.

"Do as you're told, Sam," said Sam. "Or I'll keep you in at break."

Mr Brown turned very pink, and then sat down.

Sam grinned. He liked being Headmaster!

13

Mr Brown was very cross.

He was cross in his history lesson.

He was cross

in maths.

But then it was time for PE. Mr Brown hadn't
played football since he was a little boy.
As he kicked the ball it felt ... good!

Mr Brown ran up the pitch towards the goal.

He dodged past Tommy and kicked the ball hard!

"Goal!" Mr Brown cried.

Everyone cheered.

Except Tommy.

"Foul!" Tommy cried, clutching his leg.

"Sam kicked me!"

"No I didn't!" said Mr Brown. "I didn't even touch him."

"Why do you always fib, Sam?" the PE teacher sighed. "Go to the Headmaster's office now."

"But I didn't fib!" Mr Brown cried.

He looked at Tommy, who was grinning.

Mr Brown frowned.

Sam had been right about Tommy all along.

19

Sam sat in the Headmaster's office watching everyone playing football. He sighed. He wished he could join in. Instead he had a pile of work to do. Maybe it wasn't much fun being Headmaster after all. Suddenly, there was a knock on his door.

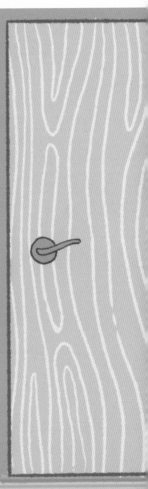

It was Mr Brown!

"I'm in trouble for kicking Tommy," Mr Brown said.

"But I didn't. Tommy likes getting other people

into trouble, doesn't he?"

Sam nodded. "Mainly me."

"I'm sorry I didn't believe you," Mr Brown said.

"That's okay," Sam said. "I'm sorry for playing pop music in assembly. I thought it would be fun being Headmaster but it is hard work. I wish we could swap back."

"Me too," Mr Brown sighed.

Just then the lunch bell rang.

"Here's your lunchbox," Mr Brown said,

passing it to Sam.

Inside was another apple!

"I wonder if this one's magic too?" Sam said,

taking a bite ...

Suddenly he was back in his own body!

Mr Brown and Sam smiled at each other and sighed with relief.

"Now I can play football again!" Sam grinned, running outside.

"Have fun," Mr Brown smiled. "I'll believe you fron now on, Sam. And I'll keep Tommy inside at lunchtime all week for fibbing."

"Thanks," Sam grinned, heading for the door.

"And Sam,?" Mr Brown said, his eyes twinkling.

"Maybe playing pop songs in assembly is

a good idea. It certainly woke everybody up, eh?"

Mr Brown winked and Sam laughed.

Gran's apple had worked!

Things to think about

1. How does Sam feel before swapping bodies with Mr Brown? How does he feel after it happens?
2. What does Mr Brown discover about Tommy while he is in Sam's body?
3. Why does Sam want to swap back to his usual self?
4. How does Mr Brown react when he and Sam have swapped back to their normal selves?
5. Can you think of any other stories in which characters swap bodies? Compare it with this story.

Write it yourself

One of the themes in this story is seeing things from someone else's point of view. Now write your own story with this theme.

Plan your story before you begin to write it.
Start off with a story map:

- a beginning to introduce the characters and where your story is set (the setting);
- a problem which the main characters will need to fix in the story;
- an ending where the problems are resolved.

Notes for parents and carers

Independent reading

This series is designed to provide an opportunity for your child to read independently, for pleasure and enjoyment. These notes are written for you to help your child make the most of this book.

About the book

When Sam takes a bite of an apple at school, something very strange happens ... he somehow swaps bodies with his headmaster, Mr Brown! At first it's a lot of fun but Sam soon wishes he could swap back!

Before reading

Ask your child why they have selected this book. Look at the title and blurb together. What do they think it will be about? Do they think they will like it?

During reading

Encourage your child to read independently. If they get stuck on a word, remind them that they can sound it out in syllable chunks. They can also read on in the sentence and think about what would make sense.

After reading

Support comprehension and help your child think about the messages in the book that go beyond the story, using the questions on the page opposite. Give your child a chance to respond to the story, asking:

- Did you enjoy the story and why?
- Who was your favourite character?
  What was your favourite part?
- What did you expect to happen at the end?

Franklin Watts
First published in Great Britain in 2020
by The Watts Publishing Group

Series Editors: Jackie Hamley and Melanie Palmer
Series Advisors: Dr Sue Bodman and Glen Franklin
Series Designers: Cathryn Gilbert and Peter Scoulding

A CIP catalogue record for this book is
available from the British Library.

ISBN 978 1 4451 7249 1 (hbk)
ISBN 978 1 4451 7254 5 (pbk)
ISBN 978 1 4451 7767 0 (library ebook)
ISBN 978 1 4451 8069 4 (ebook)

Printed in China

Franklin Watts
An imprint of
Hachette Children's Group
Part of The Watts Publishing Group
Carmelite House
50 Victoria Embankment
London EC4Y 0DZ

An Hachette UK Company
www.hachette.co.uk

www.franklinwatts.co.uk